Secret PRINCESSES

Starlight
Sleepover

ROSIE BANKS

Wishing Star Palace

The Secret Princess Promise

"I promise that I will be kind and brave,

Using my magic to help and save,

Granting wishes and doing my best,

To make people smile and bring happiness."

 # CONTENTS

CHAPTER ONE
Giant Trees

Sunlight shone through the treetops, casting pretty shadows on the forest floor. Charlotte couldn't believe how big the giant redwood trees were. They towered up into the sky, with massive green ferns growing between them. *It feels so magical here*, Charlotte thought, looking around. *A unicorn could be watching me, or a dragon!*

Up ahead of her, Liam, one of her twin little brothers, called out, "Mum! Dad! Check out this tree!"

The Williams family had only been living in California a few months but Charlotte's brothers were already starting to sound American.

Charlotte ran to join Liam. "I bet we can't get our arms all the way around it even if we all hold hands," she said. "Let's try."

Her mum, dad and Liam's twin, Harvey, hurried over

and held hands, but the tree trunk
was so thick they couldn't mange to
make a circle around it.

"We're being watched," Mr Williams
pointed out, as a chipmunk peered at them
from a nearby bush.

"They're so cute," said Charlotte as the
chipmunk scampered away.

"I hope we see a bear," said Harvey.

"If we do, I'll run!" said Liam.

"No, you mustn't," said Charlotte quickly.
"If you run it'll chase you. You've got to
make yourself seem big and make loads of
noise to scare it away."

"How do you know?" asked Liam,
sounding impressed.

Charlotte grinned. "Mia, of course." Mia was her best friend who lived in England, where Charlotte and her family came from. Mia loved animals and was always sharing interesting facts about them. Charlotte sighed. "I wish she could see all the different animals here in California."

Her mum gave her shoulder a squeeze. "It must feel like ages since you saw her."

Charlotte hid her smile. If only her mum knew! She and Mia had actually seen each other twice since she moved away. But no one else knew because it was a secret – a magical secret!

Charlotte felt a shiver of delight as she touched the gold pendant that hung around

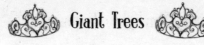

her neck. It was shaped like half a heart and had two diamonds embedded in it. Mia's pendant was the other half of the heart. When the necklaces glowed, they whisked Charlotte and Mia away to the most incredible, enchanted place in the whole world – Wishing Star Palace, the home of the Secret Princesses!

If Charlotte and Mia completed their training, one day they would become princesses too. And not just ordinary princesses – Secret Princesses used magic to grant wishes! Sometimes Charlotte had to pinch herself to believe it was true!

A spark of light flew across the pendant. Charlotte frowned. Had she imagined it?

But no! There was another! And another!

As her brothers scrambled over a fallen tree trunk, Charlotte ducked behind an enormous tree. The pendant began to sparkle and glow. Charlotte's tummy somersaulted with excitement. She was going to have an adventure!

She closed her fingers around the pendant. No time would pass while she was away, so she knew her family wouldn't be worried. "I wish that I could see Mia!" she whispered.

WHOOSH! Charlotte felt herself spinning through the air in a tunnel of brilliant golden light. As soon as her feet hit solid ground she opened her eyes.

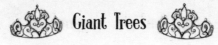

Even though she had been there twice before, the entrance hall of Wishing Star Palace was so grand it made her gasp.

She glanced down and squealed with excitement. Her shorts and T-shirt had transformed into her beautiful pink princess

dress with dark pink roses on the skirt, and she could feel her tiara sitting on her brown curls. "Yes!" she breathed, twirling around on the spot and making her pretty skirt spin out.

Charlotte gazed around the hall, looking for Mia. Though it was still beautiful, the hall – like the rest of the palace – was rather faded and shabby. Paint was peeling off the walls and some of the windows were cracked. Charlotte shivered. She knew it was all because of Princess Poison. Nasty and cruel, Princess Poison had once been a Secret Princess but had turned bad. Now, she used her magic selfishly to spoil wishes. Whenever she succeeded, the palace crumbled a little bit more.

"Charlotte!"

Charlotte spun round. Mia was running down the wide staircase, wearing a gorgeous sparkly gold princess dress and a gold tiara.

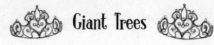
Her long blonde hair was
up in a pretty bun.

"Mia!" Charlotte cried.

They hugged at the
bottom of the stairs.

Mia looked
around. "It's
very quiet
here today,
isn't it?"

Charlotte
nodded.

"I wonder where everyone is?" Both the
other times they had come to the palace
there had been lots of other Secret
Princesses around.

She opened a door leading into a large ballroom and peeked in. It had a shiny marble floor and rich velvet curtains hanging from its tall windows, but there was nobody inside. "Strange." The huge kitchen, full of gleaming copper pots and pans, was deserted too.

"There's no one upstairs, either." Mia looked worried. "You don't think something bad happened, do you? Remember Princess Poison told us she was going to turn Wishing Star Palace into Poison Palace!"

"She can't have done," said Charlotte, hoping she was right. "Come on," she said, taking Mia's hand. "Let's find out what's going on!"

CHAPTER TWO
Party Time

Charlotte and Mia opened the palace doors
and hurried outside. Where was everyone?

Wishing Star Palace and its gorgeous
gardens rested on a bed of fluffy white
clouds. The trees looked like they were
covered in brightly coloured blossoms, but
they weren't flowers – they were candyfloss
and lollipops! Charlotte's mouth watered at

the thought, but there was no time to taste them today. They needed to find the Secret Princesses!

Mia suddenly pointed across the lawn. "Look over there!"

Charlotte sighed in relief. Across the garden were the princesses, sitting on blankets and tucking into an amazing, delicious-looking picnic.

A princess in a red dress who had wavy, strawberry-blonde hair saw them. "Mia! Charlotte!" she cried, waving. "Over here!"

The girls waved back and ran over. It was their old friend, Alice De Silver. Alice had given them both their magic necklaces just before Charlotte had moved to America.

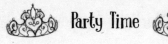

She had once been the girls' babysitter but was now a pop star back in the real world. And at Wishing Star Palace she was a Secret Princess, of course!

"Come and sit down!" called Princess Sylvie, who had a green dress and a pendant shaped like a cupcake, showing her special talent for baking. Her deep red hair was piled up in a bun. "You're just in time to have some of my special cake."

"It looks amazing!" said Charlotte.

The five-tiered cake in the middle of the picnic blanket was almost as tall as Mia and Charlotte! Each layer was iced in a different colour – lilac, pink, lemon yellow, mint green and pale blue – and it was decorated

with a marzipan easel and paint palette.

"Mmm – it smells delicious!" said Mia.

Alice handed them both glasses of fizzy pink lemonade. "Princess Sylvie made it because it's five years exactly since Princess Sophie had her Princess Ceremony and became a full Secret Princess," she said.

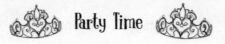

Princess Sophie, an artist who had a paintbrush pendant on her necklace, smiled at the girls. "It won't be too long before you two have your own Princess Ceremonies."

"We've still got a long way to go with our training," said Mia. "We haven't even earned our proper tiaras yet."

The tiaras that Mia and Charlotte wore at Wishing Star Palace were plain gold. Once they had earned four diamonds by making four wishes come true, their tiaras would become beautiful jewelled tiaras, taking them one step closer to becoming full Secret Princesses.

"But we *will* earn them," said Charlotte, hugging Mia, "as well as all the other princess things we need."

"And then you'll both be Friendship

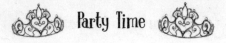

Princesses," said Alice, with a smile.

Charlotte felt a warm glow inside her. Friendship Princesses were a very rare and powerful type of Secret Princess – and they always worked in pairs. The only thing better than training to be a princess was doing it with her best friend!

"You're both doing so well," said Princess Sylvie. "Thanks to you, two of the turrets have been mended." The girls followed her gaze and saw that although two of the palace turrets were covered with moss and had missing tiles, the other two turrets sparkled and glowed in the sunlight.

"Every wish you grant repairs the palace even more," said Alice.

Charlotte couldn't wait to help someone else and fix the palace a bit more!

"But you'll need to be careful," Alice added. "Princess Poison was furious when you stopped her last time. She's bound to try and stop you from granting someone else's wish."

"We won't let her," said Charlotte, lifting her chin.

"Cake time, everyone!" Princess Sylvie trilled. She started handing out slices. The cake was as tasty as it looked – and it was magical, too. With every bite it changed flavour from chocolate to strawberry to vanilla to apricot to toffee.

As they ate, Mia looked at the gardens.

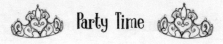

"The flowers are beautiful," she said.

Alice smiled. "Princess Evie has been looking after them. In fact, she's just grown some new flowers. Come and see!"

Charlotte and Mia followed her to a flowerbed blooming with pink and purple flowers. Mia bent down to sniff a rose. "Mmm!" she sighed, as she inhaled the heavenly scent. "It smells like … chocolate?"

"I'll show you why," Alice said, chuckling. Gently opening the rose's petals, she revealed a perfect rose-shaped chocolate nestled inside. "Try one," she said, offering it to Mia.

"That's so cool!" Charlotte exclaimed.

She opened the petals of another rose and popped the chocolate in her mouth. "I wish we had flowers like this at home!" she said, savouring the creamy chocolate.

Just then a fluffy black kitten peeped out from behind the flowerbed and miaowed. The kitten's collar had a pawprint charm on it that looked familiar.

Mia bent down and scooped it up. It licked her cheek with its little pink tongue and she giggled.

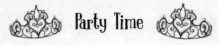

"It's so cute!" Charlotte exclaimed.

The kitten purred.

"He belongs to Princess Ella," said Alice. "Should we take him back to her? She's looking after the horses."

"Horses?" gasped Mia. "I didn't know you had horses here!"

"Oh, yes," said Alice. "Why don't you come and meet them?"

She led the way through the gardens to an old stone stableyard at the back of the palace. The stables were arranged around a courtyard with a fountain in the middle. Bright hanging baskets hung by each stable door. Beautiful horses looked out, whickering to the girls.

"Oh, wow," breathed Mia.

One of the stable doors opened and Princess Ella came out. She was wearing red wellies under her blue princess dress and the pendant on her necklace matched the one on the kitten's collar. "Hello, girls!" She saw the kitten in Mia's arms. "Oh, you found Sooty. He's a little scamp. Thanks for bringing him back."

Charlotte went over to the nearest stable.

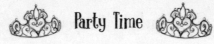

A golden horse with a long white mane and tail was looking out. "You're lovely," she said, as it nuzzled her.

"All of the horses here are very friendly," said Ella. "Would you like to have a ride?"

Charlotte and Mia glanced at each other in delight. "Yes, please!" they chorused.

Princess Ella tacked up the golden horse, called Sunbeam, for Charlotte, and then a pure-white horse, called Snowdrop, for Mia.

They tucked their skirts around their legs and cantered around a large meadow beside the stable.

"This is so fun!" Charlotte whooped.

"Do you want to do something even more fun?" Princess Ella asked, mischievously.

"Like what?" said Charlotte.

"This!" Princess Ella declared with a wave of her wand. A golden gleam ran across Snowdrop and Sunbeam's bodies and then suddenly both horses grew big, golden, feathery wings. Their wings beat up and down and the next moment they were soaring up into the sky!

"Oh, my goodness!" gasped Mia, hanging onto Snowdrop's long mane. "We're flying!"

Party Time

"This is awesome!" cried Charlotte.

"Faster, Sunbeam! Faster!"

Mia was happy to just fly in circles but
Charlotte and Sunbeam zoomed up high.

Charlotte laughed in delight as they flew a loop the loop, her brown curls streaming out behind her.

"So, do you like our horses?" Alice asked the girls, when they finally landed.

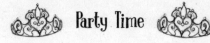

"They're amazing!" said Mia, her eyes sparkling. "I love them!" She reached over and hugged Snowdrop's neck.

"Flying's wonderful," agreed Charlotte. "I wish I could do it every day."

Sunbeam snorted. Princess Ella grinned. "I bet Sunbeam would love that too!"

As she laughed, a flash of light sparkled in the pawprint at the end of her wand.

Charlotte gasped. "Princess Ella, your wand – it's glowing!"

"Yours too, Alice!" said Mia, pointing to the musical note at the end of Alice's wand. It was shining brightly.

Charlotte looked at Mia, and she grinned back, her eyes dancing with excitement.

They both knew what that meant!

"Someone has a wish that needs granting," said Princess Ella.

"Are you two ready to have another adventure?" Alice asked.

Charlotte and Mia looked at each other. "Let's go!" they cried.

CHAPTER THREE
Camp Sunshine

Mia, Charlotte and Alice ran to the palace and dashed up a spiral staircase, taking the stairs two at a time. They reached the top of the turret and burst into the Mirror Room, panting. It was empty apart from an oval mirror in a tarnished stand.

Charlotte and Mia touched the magic glass. Light ran across the cloudy surface

 39

and then a rhyme floated across it.
Charlotte read it out:

"Your magic training is underway.
Someone needs your help today,
Each wish you grant, a diamond
you will own –
Four will give you your princess crown!"

"Let's find out who needs our help." Alice
touched her wand to the mirror. The rhyme
was replaced by the image of a girl. She
was sitting on a bunk bed in a wooden
cabin. Her face was buried in her hands,
her shoulder-length, blonde hair falling
over her fingers.

New words swirled up under the image.

"A wish needs granting, adventures await,
Call Laura's name, don't hesitate!"

Alice looked at them. "Are you girls both ready?"

Mia nodded. "Let's go quickly. She looks really sad."

"Good luck," Alice said. "If you work together I'm sure you'll be able to help Laura. Just remember to watch out for Princess Poison!"

Charlotte took Mia's hand. "After three. One, two, three …"

"Laura!" they both said together.

The mirror swirled with light again, making a golden tunnel that sucked them inside. They shot down it like a water flume.

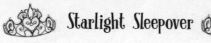

"Wheee!" Charlotte cried, as they tumbled out the other end. As she blinked her eyes in the bright sunshine, she saw that their princess dresses had changed into pretty shorts and T-shirts. "Awesome!" she said, twirling round to show Mia her new outfit.

They were standing in a large clearing in a forest. It was surrounded by lots of wooden cabins,

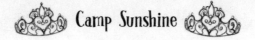

and overhead hung a big banner that read, 'Welcome to Camp Sunshine!'

"We're at a summer camp," said Charlotte. Lots of her new school friends had told her they were going to summer camp. The pictures they'd shown her looked just like this.

Girls and boys were hanging around outside the cabins, chatting and laughing. For a moment, Charlotte worried about how they'd explain their sudden arrival from out of nowhere. Then she remembered how wish magic worked – nobody would notice anything out of the ordinary.

"Where do you think Laura is?" said Mia, looking around.

Charlotte went to the window of the cabin and peeped inside. Laura was sitting sadly on one of the bunks. "In here," Charlotte said.

She knocked on the door.

"Come in," a small voice said.

Charlotte opened the door.

"If you're looking for Lily, Amelia and Ruby, they've gone to explore," Laura said in a small, snuffly voice.

"We're not looking for them. We wanted to come and meet you," said Charlotte, stepping inside. "I'm Charlotte and this is my best friend, Mia."

"Are you from one of the other cabins?" Laura asked.

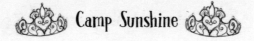

"Um … no," Mia said.

"We're – er – just visiting," said Charlotte.

"Oh, right." Laura bit her lip. "Well, hi. I'm Laura."

"Are you OK?" Mia asked her gently.

Laura shook her head, a tear rolling down her cheek.

Charlotte gave Mia a worried look. She never really knew what to do when people cried. But Mia hurried over and sat next to Laura. She put her hand on her arm. "What's wrong? Come on, you can tell us."

Laura sniffed. "It's really silly but, well, I'm so homesick. I've never been away from my family before. My big sister said camp's great but I don't know anybody. I wish I had some friends here." She stopped and blushed. "Sorry, I don't know why I'm telling you this."

Charlotte caught Mia's eye again. Mia looked as concerned as Charlotte felt – they had to help Laura!

"Don't worry," said Charlotte, coming

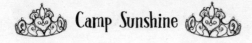

and sitting on the other side of Laura.

"We might be able to help," said Mia.

Charlotte nodded. "And you *do* have friends here."

"That's right," Mia agreed, nodding. "You've got us."

"Thanks," said Laura shyly.

Just then a whistle blasted outside. Charlotte glanced out of the window. Everyone seemed to be heading over to the centre of the camp. She opened the door and Mia and Laura followed her outside.

Three camp counsellors were standing in the middle of the clearing. They were all wearing green T-shirts with big round suns on them.

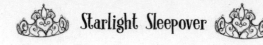
"That's it, everyone. Gather round!" the lady counsellor called. "My name is Kelli-Anne and these guys are Adam and Brad. We'll be in charge of the first fun activity today, which is den building!"

There was a chorus of cheers.

Adam stepped forward. "Right, everyone, get into teams and work together. You can use anything you find in the woods to make your dens."

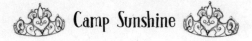

"And there'll be a prize for the best one," Brad added. "So let's go!"

Everyone started splitting into groups. "Should we be a team?" Laura asked Charlotte and Mia.

"Yes. But let's find a few others, too," said Charlotte.

"Those girls are in my cabin," said Laura, pointing to a group of girls nearby.

Mia gave Charlotte a hopeful look. Charlotte knew that Mia would be too shy to approach a group of girls she didn't know. Luckily, Charlotte wasn't shy at all! "Hi, there," she called, going up to them. "I'm Charlotte. I'm friends with Laura from your cabin and this is my other friend, Mia.

Do you want to make a den together?"

"Yeah, sure!" One of the girls grinned at them. She had dark skin like Charlotte and her curly black hair was cut into a bob. "I'm Lily. And this is Ruby and Amelia."

Ruby was tall and slim with thick blonde curls caught back in a ponytail. Amelia had long, brown hair with a fringe and green eyes. They both smiled in a friendly way.

"Is anyone here good at making dens?" Charlotte asked.

"Only the sort you make indoors with a blanket," said Amelia, with a giggle.

"My team made a really good one last year," said Lily. "We built it around the trunk of a tree so it didn't collapse."

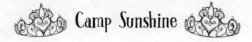

Charlotte glanced at Laura. She was standing on the edge of the group, not saying a word. "How about you, Laura? Have you ever built a den?"

"Um … yes," Laura said. "My grandpa taught me and my sister how to build dens when we were little. We always used to cover the roof with leaves and moss."

"That's a great idea!" said Lily.

"Cool. Let's get started!" said Charlotte.

They set off into the forest and got to work. Laura and Lily choose a big, solid tree trunk while Charlotte, Mia, Amelia and Ruby gathered branches. Working together, they leaned the branches against the tree trunk so that they made a teepee shape.

Once the walls were in place they all
fetched moss and leaves
for the roof.
It was lots
of fun.

"Almost
done!"
said Laura
as she
dragged
some small
logs into the den for seats.

"I think our den's the best," said Ruby
looking round.

"It's great," agreed Amelia, admiring it.

"We just need more moss," said Laura,

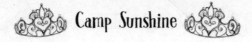

pushing clumps of moss into a few remaining holes.

A camp counsellor came over. He was small and had a baseball cap pulled down low over his face, which was hidden behind a clipboard. His Camp Sunshine T-shirt strained over his round tummy. Charlotte stared at him – she didn't remember seeing him with the other counsellors earlier.

He stood behind Laura, who was balancing on tiptoe as she patted the moss in place. "This den looks interesting. Let me take a closer look ..."

He leaned forward – and bumped straight into Laura! She gave a shriek as she fell heavily on to the den. Branches cracked and the whole den collapsed to the ground with Laura on top of it.

All the girls gasped in horror, and Lily, Amelia and Ruby rushed forward to help Laura up.

"What happened?" Ruby asked Laura as she got back to her feet.

"I ... I must have lost my balance," she said with a wail.

"What a shame!" said the counsellor, not sounding sorry at all. "You should try being less clumsy."

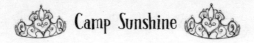

Ruby ignored him. "The most important thing is that you're OK, Laura."

"I am but ..." Laura's eyes filled with tears. "Look at our den – it's ruined!"

"Don't worry," said Amelia. "We can rebuild it. Come on!" She and the others started to pick up the branches.

"You're not going to have enough time. There's only ten minutes left before the judging starts," said the counsellor. "Oh dear, it looks like your den is going to come last." He sniggered.

Charlotte frowned. He was being very mean and there was something familiar about his voice. She marched over to him and pulled up his baseball cap.

"Hex!" she cried, recognising Princess
Poison's horrible servant.

He smirked at her, then hurried off to
inspect another den.

Mia had recognised the little man too.
She pulled Charlotte over to one side. "Hex
must have pushed Laura on purpose!" she
whispered.

"She's really upset," said Charlotte,
seeing tears streaking down Laura's face.
"We've got to do something!" Her eyes
caught a flash of light. Mia's pendant was
glowing! Glancing down, she saw that her
own pendant was shining too. She grinned.
"You know what?" she said. "I think it's time
for some wish magic!"

CHAPTER FOUR
River Ride

Charlotte and Mia hurried back to where
the other girls were rebuilding the den.
"Lots of the branches are broken," said
Ruby, as they arrived.

"Why don't Mia, Laura and I tidy up here
and the rest of you go and find some more
branches?" Charlotte suggested. "If we work
together, I'm sure we can mend it in time."

They nodded and set off into the trees.

Laura looked very downcast. "I'm so clumsy," she said.

"It wasn't your fault," said Mia. "That mean counsellor bumped into you."

"We can help fix the den," said Charlotte. "We can make it as good as new by the time the others come back."

"How?" asked Laura.

"By using magic," Mia whispered.

"Magic?" Laura exclaimed.

Mia nodded. "I know it's hard to believe, but Charlotte and I aren't campers – we're training to be Secret Princesses."

"We grant wishes using magic," Charlotte added quickly, seeing the confusion on

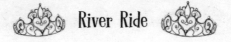

Laura's face. "But you mustn't tell anyone else about us."

Laura looked like she didn't know whether to believe them or not.

"Watch," said Charlotte, knowing there was only one way to prove to Laura that what they said was true.

She and Mia fitted the two halves of their pendants together. "I wish that the den could be fixed and look even better than before!" said Charlotte.

Sparkles shot out of both their pendants and floated down on to the pile of sticks from the ruined den.

The branches shimmered, and the whole pile was covered by a golden glow. Then suddenly the den was whole again.

Laura gasped. "Oh … wow!"

The new den was round and sturdy, with pretty flowers all around it. A curtain made from woven ivy hung across the entrance, tied to one side with a ribbon. Inside, the girls could see two wooden seats made from logs, covered with velvety moss cushions.

"I can't believe it!" Laura said, astonished. "You really *can* do magic!"

"Yes, but you've got to keep it a secret," Mia told her.

"But everyone will notice when they see the new den!" said Laura.

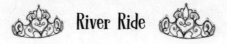

"They'll notice it," said Charlotte. "But they won't think it's strange. Thanks to the way wish magic works, the only people that will know what really happened are you, me and Mia."

Just then the other three girls came back into the clearing.

"You've been busy!" said Ruby.

"You guys fixed the den," said Amelia. "Well done!"

"Let's go inside," said Lily. They ducked under the ivy curtain and went inside the den.

Laura grinned even more and her eyes started to shine. "This is so exciting!" she whispered to Mia and Charlotte.

Lily poked
her head out.
"Aren't you
three coming
in too?"

"In a
minute," called
Charlotte. She gave
Laura a little nudge. "Go on, you join them.
I need to talk to Mia about something."

"OK," Laura said, still grinning excitedly.
She went into the den.

Mia turned to Charlotte. "What is it?"

"Princess Poison!" said Charlotte. "If Hex
is here, she's bound to be here too. We'll
have to keep a look out, Mia."

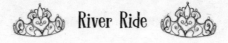

Mia shivered. "They'll probably try and stop us from granting Laura's wish."

"They can interfere all they like," Charlotte declared. "But there's no way they're going to stop us from helping Laura."

Mia nodded determinedly. "No way at all."

The girls were all delighted when their den was announced the winner. As a prize, they were given a big bag of sweets to share after their lunch. Their group ate inside their cosy den. As they munched hot dogs

and sipped cups of fruit punch, they told
each other about their families and friends
back at home.

Then a whistle blew and the girls
returned to the clearing.

"Right! Your afternoon activity is a canoe
trip," Kelli-Anne announced.

"You all need to wear life jackets," Brad
said. "And there should be six people per
boat. One of you needs to navigate – the
rest can paddle."

The girls ran down to the river to where
Adam was handing out lifejackets. "Are you
six going together?" he asked.

They all nodded. Adam helped them into
a canoe.

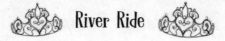

"Why don't you steer, Laura?" Charlotte suggested.

"Um … does anyone else want to?" Laura asked, but everyone shook their heads.

"No, you do it," said Ruby.

"I'd be useless!" said Lily.

They all clambered in and Laura sat at the back, behind Charlotte and Mia. The canoe started floating down the peaceful, gently flowing river. On either bank, trees dipped their branches into the water.

As the girls paddled along, a bright blue bird flew over the water.

"A kingfisher!" said Laura and Amelia at the same time. They smiled at each other.

"I'm crazy about animals," said Laura.

"Me too," said Amelia, pointing to the shore. "Look, can you see that deer watching us from the trees?"

"I think it's a black-tailed deer," said Laura as they all looked at the wild deer. "You can tell because it has big ears and a black tail."

"It looks a bit like Bambi," said Lily.

Charlotte grinned. "What do you get if you cross Bambi with a ghost?"

"What?" asked Laura.

"Bam-BOO!" Charlotte said.

They all giggled.

As Amelia, Laura and Mia chatted about animals, Charlotte dug her paddle into the water in a regular rhythm. She felt a warm flush of contentment as they floated downstream. Laura seemed happier already.

She had started making friends. Maybe they wouldn't even need to use any more of their wishes …

"Hey, who's in that canoe?" said Ruby, pointing to a canoe that was heading straight towards them. There was a scary face painted on the front of the boat that made it look like a sea monster.

"Isn't that the mean counsellor who

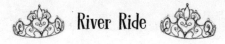

bumped into Laura?" said Amelia.

Charlotte felt her heart sink. Hex was paddling the canoe towards them and behind him sat a tall, skinny figure. Her long black hair had an ice-blonde streak. She was wearing a spangled green jumpsuit that was far too glamorous for canoeing. It was Princess Poison!

Beside her, Mia gasped. "Oh, no!"

"We'd better steer to the right," said
Laura. "We don't want to crash into them."

Everyone started paddling on the left to
turn the canoe away, but Princess Poison's
canoe was speeding towards them.

"Paddle faster!" Charlotte cried.

They paddled as hard as they could,
but it was no use. Princess Poison's canoe
surged forward, powered by magic. Her boat
banged hard into theirs, making a hole.

"Yikes!" The girls cried out in alarm as
their canoe rocked violently.

"You stupid girl!" Princess Poison shouted,
pointing at Laura. "Why didn't you get
out of the way in time? Now look what
you've done."

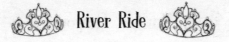

Laura shook her head. "I'm sorry! I tried to steer the other way."

"Well, you obviously didn't try hard enough," snapped Princess Poison, a mean glint in her green eyes. "This is all your fault!"

Water started pouring in through the hole, soaking the girls' feet.

"Our canoe's leaking!" gasped Lily.

"What are we going to do?" said Amelia.

"Quick! Bail the water out!" said Charlotte, glaring at Princess Poison. She knew she'd caused the accident on purpose. The water was coming in faster and faster.

"Can you help us?" Ruby called to Princess Poison.

Princess Poison's canoe started to speed down the river, though Hex was barely paddling.

"Whoops! We seem to be caught in the current!" Princess Poison said.

Hex sniggered.

"Wait!" gasped Amelia. "You can't just leave us here to sink."

"Sorry, but we're in a bit of a rush!" Princess Poison said. "I hope you don't get too wet, my sweets." She wriggled her fingers at them and smirked at Charlotte and Mia. "Toodle-oo!"

CHAPTER FIVE
Dinner Disaster

"Quick, we've got to stop the water coming in!" cried Amelia, trying to scoop some of the water out of the bottom of the canoe with her hands.

They all joined in.

"I tried to steer us away from them," said Laura. "But their canoe was going so fast."

"Don't worry about it, Laura," said Ruby.

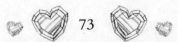

"Let's just try and get back to the bank. Maybe there'll be another boat we can use."

They paddled with all their might back towards the dock. Charlotte saw a tear roll down Laura's cheek. She looked really upset about the boat sinking.

Mia leaned closer to Charlotte. "Should we make another wish?" she breathed.

Charlotte nodded. "As soon as we get to the shore."

"Almost there!" cried Lily, grabbing a tree branch that was hanging out over the water and hauling them in. Relieved, they all climbed out onto the bank. Their shorts and trainers were soaking but the sun overhead was bright and warm and started

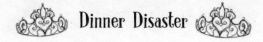

drying them straight away.

Adam came jogging over. "You guys are back early." He spotted the damaged canoe. "What happened?"

"We bumped into another boat," said Laura, hanging her head. "I couldn't steer away in time."

"Never mind," said Adam kindly. "At least you're all OK. But I'm afraid all the other boats and canoes have been taken."

Ruby, Amelia and Lily looked very disappointed.

"I'm so sorry," Laura said to them.

Mia pulled Charlotte behind the boat shed and they quickly touched their pendants together as the other girls

comforted Laura. "I wish we could find a new boat!" Mia whispered.

There was a flash of light.

Charlotte and Mia looked around. Had the magic worked? They couldn't see a boat anywhere. Suddenly, a flash of purple among the branches of a nearby weeping willow tree caught their eyes.

"What's that?" Charlotte hurried closer and pulled back the branches. "Look, everyone! It's a boat!"

Hidden under the weeping willow's branches was a beautiful gondola-style boat with pink padded seats and a purple and white striped canopy.

"It's the coolest boat ever!" said Ruby.

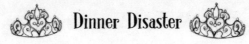

She turned to Adam. "Can we use this one?"

He shrugged. "Sure. I guess no one else noticed it under the branches."

Charlotte caught Mia's eye and winked.

Chattering excitedly, they all scrambled into the new boat and Adam pushed them downstream. "Have fun, girls!" he called after them.

"Mia and I will row," said Charlotte.

She and Mia dipped the oars into the water and the boat glided down the river.

"This is awesome!" said Lily, settling back against the cushions.

"This boat is loads better than the boring old canoe," said Amelia.

Ruby giggled. "I'm almost glad that we crashed now."

Laura smiled at Charlotte and Mia. "Thank you!" she mouthed.

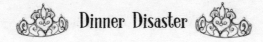
They grinned back and rowed further
down the river. On the way, they saw more
deer and kingfishers. Pretty blue butterflies
danced over the
water and a
friendly otter
swam beside
them for part of
the way. It was the
best boat trip ever!

When they finally got back to camp, they
were all very hungry. "I wonder what's for
supper?" said Ruby, just as Kelli-Anne was
passing by.

"Ah, girls," the counsellor said, "I'm
looking for some volunteers to make supper.

Would you like to help? There'll be extra
marshmallows for you to toast around the
campfire if you do!"

"I'll do it," said Ruby eagerly. "I love
cooking."

"Me too," said Laura.

"And me," said Mia.

"I'm not very good at cooking, but I'll do
anything for marshmallows," said Amelia.

"Let's all do it. It'll be fun," said
Charlotte.

"That's the Camp Sunshine spirit!" said
Kelli-Anne, beaming. "Come with me!"

She took them into the main building
and showed them the kitchen. "Tonight
we're having sausage and bean casserole,"

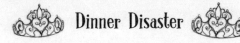

she said. "There are some recipe books over on the shelf."

"We don't need a recipe. My mum makes a great sausage and bean casserole," said Laura. "I know how to do it."

"Great! I'll leave you to it then. Give me a shout if you need help!" Kelli-Anne hurried out, her short hair bouncing on her shoulders.

"So, what do we do?" said Charlotte.

"Well, we need to chop up some celery and onions first. Then we'll add tins of beans and tomatoes and sausages," said Laura.

"We could maybe make a crunchy topping for it, too," suggested Ruby.

"Definitely!" said Laura. "Let's get started."

Soon they were all busy chopping and cooking. Laura and Ruby organised everyone. They debated how

much salt and pepper to use and whether they should add mushrooms or not. By the time the casserole was in the oven in two enormous pots, the kitchen was filled with a

delicious scent of cooking, and the sun was setting outside.

"Everyone's going to love this casserole," said Ruby.

"It's perfect for our first night at camp," said Lily.

"I'm going to toast loads of marshmallows on the campfire," said Amelia.

"I can't wait to stay up late and tell stories in our cabin," said Ruby. "What are you looking forward to, Laura?"

"Um." Laura swallowed. "I … I don't know. I've never been away to camp before, you see." She wrapped her arms around herself. "I'm worried that I'm going to miss my family at night."

"You'll be fine," Ruby said kindly. "You'll have us."

"Yeah, we'll look after you," said Lily.

"We promise you won't be lonely," added Amelia. "Look, why don't we go and finish unpacking? We can make our cabin look really cosy."

Charlotte and Mia exchanged a grin as Laura's new friends reassured her.

"But what about Charlotte and Mia?" said Laura.

"Don't worry about us," said Charlotte quickly. "We'll stay here and look after all the food."

"We'll be back soon. Thanks," said Lily.

Laura went off arm in arm with her

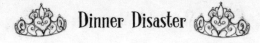

bunkmates. Mia smiled at Charlotte. "You know, I think Laura's wish to make friends at camp is going to come true."

"Oh, no, it isn't!" a voice snapped.

Charlotte and Mia jumped back as Princess Poison strode into the kitchen. She slammed the door shut behind her. "So, you think you're

going to make that silly girl's wish come true, do you?" she taunted. "Well, think again!"

Mia shrank back but Charlotte was too cross to be scared. "You haven't stopped us yet and you're not going to now!" she said, putting her hands on her hips. "We're going

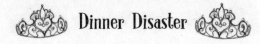

to grant Laura's wish and get our third diamond. Then we'll just need to grant one more wish to complete the first stage of our training and get our full princess tiaras!"

"Tiaras!" Princess Poison laughed nastily. "You'll never get those. Oh, no – Laura's going to be lonely and friendless at camp."

"No, she won't!" said Mia angrily. "She's already starting making friends!"

"Ha!" Princess Poison snorted. "Let's see if they like her so much when the whole camp is forced to eat her disgusting casserole!"

"Her casserole isn't disgusting. It's delicious!" exclaimed Charlotte.

Princess Poison cackled. "I think you mean it WAS delicious!" She cackled nastily, then pointed her wand at the oven and shouted:

**"Bubble and boil, Laura's stew
Turn to rotten eggs and glue!"**

A green bolt of lightning hit the oven door. The two casserole pots glowed bright green and immediately started smoking. A horrible smell of rotten eggs filled the air.

"Let's see how many people want to be Laura's friend after eating that!" shrieked Princess Poison, before sweeping out of the kitchen and into the night.

CHAPTER SIX
Cooking Catastrophe

Mia ran to the oven. Coughing and spluttering, she used the oven gloves to take the casseroles out. She lifted the lids and reeled back as an even stinkier smell filled the room. "Oh, no. Look at them!"

Charlotte's heart pounded. The casserole was now a mix of mouldy black and green scrambled eggs and blobs of thick glue.

89

"What are we going to do?" Mia said

The door opened. For a moment, Charlotte thought Princess Poison was back, but it was Laura.

She smiled shyly. "Hi, I just wanted to say thank you for helping me make—" Laura broke off as the foul odour hit her. "Ugh! What's that gross smell?" Before the girls could answer, her eyes fell on the casseroles. "What happened?" she cried.

"Laura, we're really sorry but the casseroles are ruined," said Mia.

Laura ran to the casseroles. "Oh, no! Everyone's going to hate me because it was my recipe. How did this happen?"

"It was wish magic – but not the good

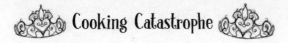
sort," said Charlotte grimly.

"But don't worry," Mia said suddenly. "It's not too late to fix it. We've still got one wish left." She grabbed her pendant. It was glowing faintly. Just then the dinner gong rang outside. "Come on, Charlotte! There's no time to lose! Otherwise there will be nothing to eat for supper."

Charlotte ran to her and they fitted the two half-hearts together. "I wish for a delicious meal for the campers!" she cried.

Laura squealed as sparkles shot out of the heart and swirled around the room. They spun faster and faster and then in a bright flash of light the mouldy, burnt casseroles disappeared and a new spread

of food appeared on the table. There were juicy burgers, corn on the cob smothered in butter, baked potatoes stuffed with cheese, a new stew brimming with sausages and beans and bowls of crispy salad.

"Oh, wow!" said Laura. "That's amazing!"

Just then Kelli-Anne came bouncing into the kitchen. "Oh, my! What a sight!" she exclaimed. "You guys have done an awesome job!"

Chattering and laughing, campers spilled out of their cabins and headed to the dining tables. They all exclaimed in delight as they saw the food waiting for them.

"This smells amazing!"

"Yum! Look at all this!"

"Burgers – my favourite!"

Ruby, Amelia and Lily joined Laura.

"Wow, we really make a great team, don't we?" Ruby said.

"You'd better watch out, I'll be asking you to cook supper everyday," said Kelli-Anne with a grin, as she handed out cutlery.

Everyone piled their plates high with food then chatted as they ate it at long dining tables. Charlotte and Mia tucked into the food along with everyone else.

After they had finished eating, Kelli-Anne announced, "Listen up, campers! Change into your pyjamas then come back outside for a starlight sing-along around the campfire."

"What are we going to do?" Charlotte whispered, pulling Mia to the side as the campers trooped back to their cabins. "We haven't got any pyjamas."

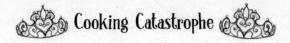

Mia looked worried. "If we stay in these clothes, everyone will know we're not really campers."

Charlotte thought fast. "Would you like Mia and me to do the washing up?" she asked Kelli-Anne.

"It's kind of you to offer. But you've done so much already…" said Kelli-Anne.

"It's no problem," said Charlotte, grabbing Mia's hand and dragging her towards the kitchen.

"So, why are we washing up?" Mia asked, giving her a confused look as they reached the kitchen.

"So Kelli-Anne and the other counsellors don't realise that we're not really campers.

It'll give us time to work out what to do about not having pyjamas."

"Good plan," said Mia.

There was a cackle of laughter as Princess Poison and Hex suddenly appeared in the kitchen in a cloud of green smoke.

"Or maybe not. How about I tell everyone that you're not campers?" she said. "That's a much better plan." A gloating expression crossed her face. "Yes, I think it's about time you two got lost. Then Hex and I will make sure that girl is miserable." She hooked a long, green-polished nail under Mia's necklace and peered at it. "Oh, dear. It's not glowing at all. You haven't got any wishes left now to stop me, have you?"

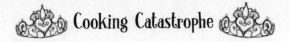

Her eyes glinted.

"Maybe we should put creepy-crawlies in everyone's beds and Laura could get the blame?" Hex suggested. "Or perhaps I could tell her a story so scary she cries and everyone thinks she's a baby—"

"Excellent suggestions," sniggered Princess Poison, letting go of Mia's necklace. "But I was thinking of having a skunk spray her, making her so stinky that nobody can stand to be around her!"

Charlotte was about to yell at them when, to her surprise, Mia stepped forward. "Go ahead and do all those mean things," she declared. Her voice was a bit shaky but she didn't back down. "It won't stop people being friends

with Laura. That's not how friendship works. If someone's your friend, they stand by you no matter what."

"Go, Mia!" whooped Charlotte. She turned to Princess Poison. "Mia's right. Laura's made friends with everyone in her cabin and that isn't going to change, no matter what you say or do." She shook her head. "You really have no clue about friendship."

"Friendship!" spat Princess Poison. Hex pulled a face.

"Maybe you two should stop being mean and try making friends," Charlotte said.

"You might actually like it," said Mia.

Princess Poison's face screwed up in scorn. "I don't need friends – I've got magic."

"Well, we've got both," said Charlotte, linking arms with Mia. "And friendship is even more powerful than magic."

"Why don't you join us by the campfire for the sing-song?" said Mia, hearing the sound of guitars starting to play. "You could start making friends there."

Princess Poison looked disgusted. She started backing away, pulling Hex with her. "Pah! I can't think of anything worse!"

"Me either!" said Hex, backing away

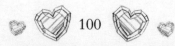

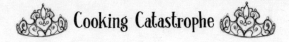

so fast that he bumped into a table and knocked over a pile of dirty pots and dishes.

Princess Poison gave a shriek as a plate of stew splattered all over her jumpsuit. "You big clumsy idiot!" she cried, throwing the plate at Hex's face.

Charlotte looked at Mia. "Oh, dear, they really aren't any good at being friends, are they?" she said. "In fact, Princess Poison is acting quite *stew*-pid!"

"Go and sing your silly little songs," snarled Princess Poison. "But don't think you've heard the last of me!" Pulling out her wand, she waved it and she and Hex vanished in a puff of green smoke.

CHAPTER SEVEN
Starlight Sing-along

Mia chuckled. "We did it! We beat Princess
Poison again!"

"We did," Charlotte said happily. She
looked at her clothes. "I just wish the
washing up was done and we had some
pyjamas so we could join the others around
the campfire. That would be a perfect end
to the day!"

There was a flash of light. Suddenly the plates and pans were sparkling clean and Mia and Charlotte's clothes had been transformed into pretty pyjamas with a dainty floral pattern, fluffy slippers and cosy lilac dressing gowns.

"What just happened?" gasped Mia. "Did our pendants grant another wish?"

"I don't think so." Charlotte lifted her pendant. "It's not glowing. I don't know how it happened ..."

Just then, a bubble floated up from the sink. It grew bigger and bigger, then an image appeared on its shimmering surface.

"It was Alice!" cried Mia, pointing at the enormous bubble.

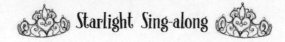

Alice's reflection
grinned and waved
at the girls.

"Thanks for your
help, Alice!" called
Charlotte.

Alice winked, then
the bubble vanished with a pop.

Mia took Charlotte's hand. "Come on!
Let's go to the campfire!"

They ran outside. All the campers were
holding fluffy marshmallows on sticks and
were toasting them in the flames of the
fire, while one of the counsellors strummed
a tune on a guitar. Laura saw Mia and
Charlotte coming and waved happily.

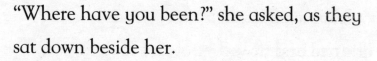

"Where have you been?" she asked, as they sat down beside her.

"Just washing up," said Mia. "Mmm, those marshmallows look good."

"Here," Laura, handing them a big pink marshmallow each.

They stuck the marshmallows on sticks and held them over the crackling flames until the outsides bubbled and turned golden brown. "Yummy!" said Charlotte, nibbling the crunchy edges of hers.

"This is so much fun," said Laura with a contented sigh.

"So you like camp now?" Mia asked.

Laura beamed, the end of her nose sticky with marshmallow. "Yes! My sister was

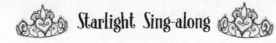
right. I've made such nice friends here. It's
like the best sleepover ever. I love it!"

A shower of shooting stars suddenly
exploded in the sky overhead. Everyone
gasped in delight as the stars zipped in
all different directions. "Shooting stars!"
Kelli-Anne cried. "Quick, make a wish,
everyone!"

All around them, people start shutting their eyes and wishing. Charlotte and Mia swapped smiles. They knew that Laura didn't need to make a wish because they'd just granted hers. As for themselves, having adventures together and training to become Secret Princesses was already a dream come true.

As the stars faded, tiny fireflies danced out from the shadow of the trees. They bobbed in the air around the campers like little sparkling globes of light.

"What song shall we sing?" said Brad, shifting his guitar on his knee. "Any suggestions?"

"We should sing one by Alice De Silver!"

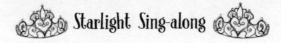

called out Charlotte.

"Great idea," said Brad. "How about 'Sunshine Friends?'" Everyone nodded. Brad strummed his guitar and a moment later the whole camp was singing Alice's latest hit. Mia snuggled closer to Charlotte and they sang along with everyone else.

As they reached the final chorus, they both heard a familiar voice singing from the trees behind them, perfectly in tune. A tingle ran down Charlotte's spine. Glancing over her shoulder, she saw Alice standing in the shadows. Charlotte nudged Mia and gestured towards Alice.

"We've got to go home now," Mia whispered to Laura.

Laura's face fell. "Do you have to?"

"Your wish is granted and we have to leave," said Charlotte. "But it's been great meeting you."

"Thank you for helping me make new friends. I'll never forget you both," Laura said.

"Enjoy the rest of camp," said Mia, and then she and Charlotte slipped away, joining Alice in the shadows of the trees.

"You've done so well, girls," Alice said. "By granting Laura's wish you've restored another of the palace's turrets. Look!"

Alice waved her wand. An image of Wishing Star Palace appeared high in the sky above them, made out of lots of tiny

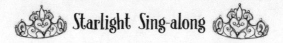

stars. It looked like a sparkling dot-to-dot picture! Three of the turrets were now glittering and glowing, completely repaired.

"But I'm forgetting something," Alice said. She touched her wand to their pendants. A third diamond magically appeared on each one, nestling besides the others. "That's for the wish you granted today. Just one more to go and you'll have earned your tiaras," Alice said.

"We'll get them!" declared Charlotte. "Nothing will stop us!"

"Not when we work together," said Mia, determination shining in her eyes.

"That's why Friendship Princesses are so special," Alice said softly. "Now it's time for you both to go home, but I'm sure we'll all meet again very soon!"

They hugged one last time and then Alice lifted her wand. A stream of sparkles shot out, surrounding both girls in a glittering, glowing cloud.

"Bye!" Charlotte gasped, as she was whisked away.

"See you soon!" the faint echo of Mia's voice floated back to her.

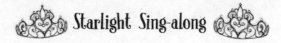

Charlotte's feet hit the ground with a soft thud. She blinked in the bright sunshine. No time had passed while she'd been away, and Charlotte found herself standing behind the giant redwood tree again.

"Charlotte!" she heard Liam calling her.

"Coming!" She darted out from behind the tree.

Liam and Harvey were scrambling over the fallen tree trunk. "Do you want to play on this with us?" Liam asked.

"I've got a better idea," said Charlotte. "Let's build a den? I'll show you how!"

Her parents sat down on a log and watched as Charlotte and her brothers gathered branches.

"This is fun!" puffed Harvey as he dragged an enormous branch over to Charlotte.

"I like building dens!" said Liam, propping the branch against a tree trunk.

Charlotte smiled. Building dens with her

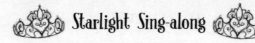

brothers *was* fun, but using magic to make a den with Mia was even better! *We'll have another adventure together soon,* thought Charlotte, her fingers closing around her pendant. *And I can't wait!*

The End

Join Charlotte and Mia in their
next Secret Princesses adventure!

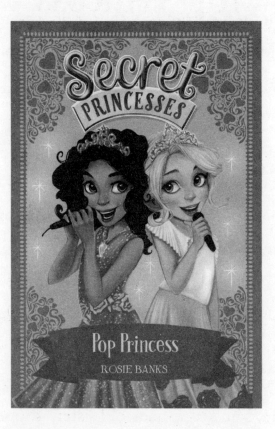

Read on for a sneak peek!

Pop Princess

"If you have friends you're never alone

   Seeing a friend is like coming home ..."

   Mia sang along to the song that was playing as she stuck glitter on a cardboard photo frame she was decorating. The song was from Alice De Silver's latest album. Alice had been Mia and her best friend Charlotte's babysitter when they were little, but now she was a famous pop star with hit songs around the world!

   Elsie, Mia's four-year-old sister, skipped into the kitchen. She had a pink tutu on

over her jeans, a silver wand in her hand
and glittery wings on her back. "I'm a fairy
ballerina!" she said, spinning around. "Look
at me, Mia."

Mia stopped singing. "You look beautiful,"
she said, smiling.

"Don't stop," Elsie said. "I like your
singing. You're so good you should be on
Talent Quest!"

Talent Quest was Mia's favourite TV
programme. She'd loved watching it ever
since Alice had been on the show two years
ago – and won!

"Sing!" Elsie commanded, tapping Mia
with her wand. "Fairy Silverwings wants
you to sing!"

"No, Elsie!" Mia said, embarrassed. She loved to sing but only when she was on her own, in a big group or with Charlotte. She was too shy to sing in front of other people, even Elsie. "Why don't you dance instead?"

Elsie didn't need any encouraging. Putting her arms above her head she twirled around the room waving her wand in time to the music, before stopping and curtseying at the end of the song.

Mia smiled and clapped. "Your dancing's getting really good."

"One day I'll be just as good as Charlotte," Elsie said. She sat down on the kitchen bench beside Mia and sighed. "I miss Charlotte. She always used to teach me cool dance steps. I wish she hadn't moved away to America."

"She's going to come back and visit one day," Mia said.

"But I want to see her *now*," Elsie said, her bottom lip sticking out.

Mia thought fast. How could she cheer up Elsie? "Hey, I've got an idea. Why don't you put another costume on and do a dance to a different Alice song?"

Elsie's face brightened. "OK!" She ran out of the kitchen to get changed.

Mia looked at the photo that she was planning to put in the frame. It was of her and Charlotte after they had been baking one day. They both had flour on their noses and huge grins as they held up a plate of cakes with rainbow-coloured sprinkles.

I'm so lucky, Mia thought and she smiled. Unlike Elsie, she didn't need to be sad about Charlotte moving away because she still got to see her. She and Charlotte shared a wonderful secret – they were training to be Secret Princesses! Just before Charlotte had moved away, Alice had given them both matching magical gold necklaces. Three times now, the necklaces had whisked Charlotte and Mia away to meet at an enchanted place called Wishing Star Palace, where they met all the Secret Princesses who used magic to make people's wishes come true!

Mia's fingers went to the necklace around her neck and she pulled the pendant out from under her T-shirt. It was in the shape of half a heart and it had three diamonds embedded in it. She and Charlotte had each been given a diamond at the end of their three adventures because they'd granted someone's wish. They just needed to earn one more diamond to pass the first stage of Secret Princess training, and then they would get beautiful jewelled tiaras to wear!

Oh, I hope we can go to Wishing Star Palace again soon, Mia thought.

The pendant started to sparkle and Mia's heart leapt. The magic was happening again! She glanced round quickly to check she was completely alone. Elsie was still getting changed. Excitement fizzed through her.

"I wish I could see Charlotte," Mia whispered quickly.

Bright light blazed out, making the cosy kitchen glow. With a delighted gasp, Mia felt herself being swept up into the light and spinning away. She was off on another magical adventure!

Read *Pop Princess* to find out what happens next!

The Secret Princess Quiz

What gift would you love to receive for your birthday?

A. A pretty cake stand.

B. A set of watercolour paints.

C. A new watering can.

What is your favourite colour?

A. Pale pink.

B. You love all colours – the brighter, the better!

C. Grassy green.

What part of Wishing Star Palace would you like to visit most?

A. The big, sparkling kitchen.

B. The light, sunny drawing room.

C. The huge, beautiful gardens.

Mostly As

You are most like Princess Sylvie! She bakes magical cakes and other delicious treats. The symbol on her pendant is a cupcake.

The Secret Princesses are all kind, helpful and brave – and each one has a special talent, too. Take this quiz to find out which princess you are most like!

If your friend is upset, what would you do to cheer them up?

A. Bake them their favourite biscuits.

B. Paint them a bright, colourful picture.

C. Pick them a bouquet of flowers.

What item of clothing couldn't you live without?

A. Apron.

B. Smock.

C. Wellies.

What's your favourite way to spend a day out?

A. Visiting a food market and tasting yummy treats.

B. Getting inspired by a trip to an art museum.

C. Picking wildflowers on a country walk.

Mostly Bs

You are most like Princess Sophie! She is an artist who loves painting portraits of her princess friends.

Mostly Cs

You are most like Princess Evie! She has a talent for gardening and loves flowers and nature.

♥ # FREE NECKLACE ♥

In every book of Secret Princesses series one: The Diamond Collection, there is a special Wish Token. Collect all four tokens to get an exclusive Best Friends necklace by

MONSOON

CHILDREN

for you and your best friend!

Simply fill in the form below, send it in with your four tokens and we'll send you your special necklaces.*

Send to: Secret Princesses Wish Token Offer, Hachette Children's Books Marketing Department, Carmelite House, 50 Victoria Embankment, London, EC4Y 0DZ

Closing Date: 31st December 2016

secretprincessesbooks.co.uk

✂

ase complete using capital letters (UK and Republic of Ireland idents only)

RST NAME:

RNAME:

TE OF BIRTH: DD | MM | YYYY

DDRESS LINE 1:

DDRESS LINE 2:

DDRESS LINE 3:

STCODE:

RENT OR GUARDIAN'S EMAIL ADDRESS:

I'd like to receive regular Secret Princesses email newsletters and information about other great Hachette Children's Group offers (I can unsubscribe at any time).

I'd like to receive regular Monsoon Children email newsletters (I can unsubscribe at any time).

Terms and Conditions apply. For full terms and conditions please go to secretprincessesbooks.co.uk/terms

1 Secret Princesses Wish Token

* 2000 necklace available while stocks last Terms and conditions apply.

Secret
PRINCESSES

What would you wish for?

Are you a Secret Princess?

Join the Secret Princesses Club at:

secretprincessesbooks.co.uk

Explore the magic of the
Secret Princesses and discover:

♥ Special competitions! ♥
♥ Exclusive content! ♥
♥ All the latest princess news! ♥